The Big Race

Written by
Barbara Gregorich

Illustrated by
Barbara Alexander

Jace looks just like Mace.

Mace looks just like Jace.

Jace and Mace
do not like Ace.

"Ha, ha! Jace and Mace have a funny face!" laughs Ace.

"Mace looks like he came from outer space," says Ace.

"Jace cannot even tie
a shoelace!" laughs Ace.

"Mace and Jace cannot race," shouts Ace.

"I can race, Ace!" says Mace.
"I will race you any place!"

"I will race you to my place," says Ace. So they begin to race.

Ace can really race!
He will beat Mace to his place.

**But wait!
Look at Jace!**

What is wrong with Jace?
Does Jace think he is Mace?

Jace will catch Ace.
Race, Jace, race!

"Oh, no! Mace wins the race!"
shouts Ace. "I will hide my face!"

They tricked Ace
and left no trace.